Library of Congress
Cataloging-in-Publication Data
Chedru, Delphine. Spot it! : find the hidden
creatures / written and illustrated by Delphine Chedru.
p. cm.   1. Picture puzzles—Juvenile literature.   I. Title.
GV1507.P47C44 2009   793.73—dc22   2008032549
ISBN 978-0-8109-0632-7
Originally published in France in 2008 by Naïve Livres under the title
Cherche la petite bête
Text and illustrations copyright © 2008 Naïve Livres, Paris
Published in 2009 by Abrams Books for Young Readers, an imprint of Harry
N. Abrams, Inc. All rights reserved. No portion of this book may be reproduced,
stored in a retrieval system, or transmitted in any form or by any means, mechanical,
electronic, photocopying, recording, or otherwise, without written permission
from the publisher.
Printed and bound in Malaysia
10 9 8 7 6 5 4 3 2 1
Abrams Books for Young Readers are available at special discounts
when purchased in quantity for premiums and promotions
as well as fundraising or educational use. Special editions
can also be created to specification. For details,
contact specialmarkets@hnabooks.com
or the address below.

HNA ▮▯▮▯▮

harry n. abrams, inc. a subsidiary of La Martinière Groupe
115 West 18th Street, New York, NY 10011. www.hnabooks.com

SPOT IT!

Find the Hidden Creatures

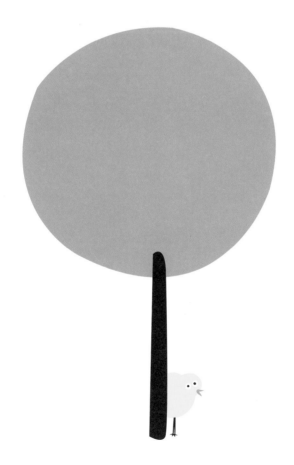

Delphine Chedru

Abrams Books for Young Readers, New York

Find the owl
who needs her glasses ...

The lost chick …

The leaping dragon . . .

The peacock
showing off his feathers . . .

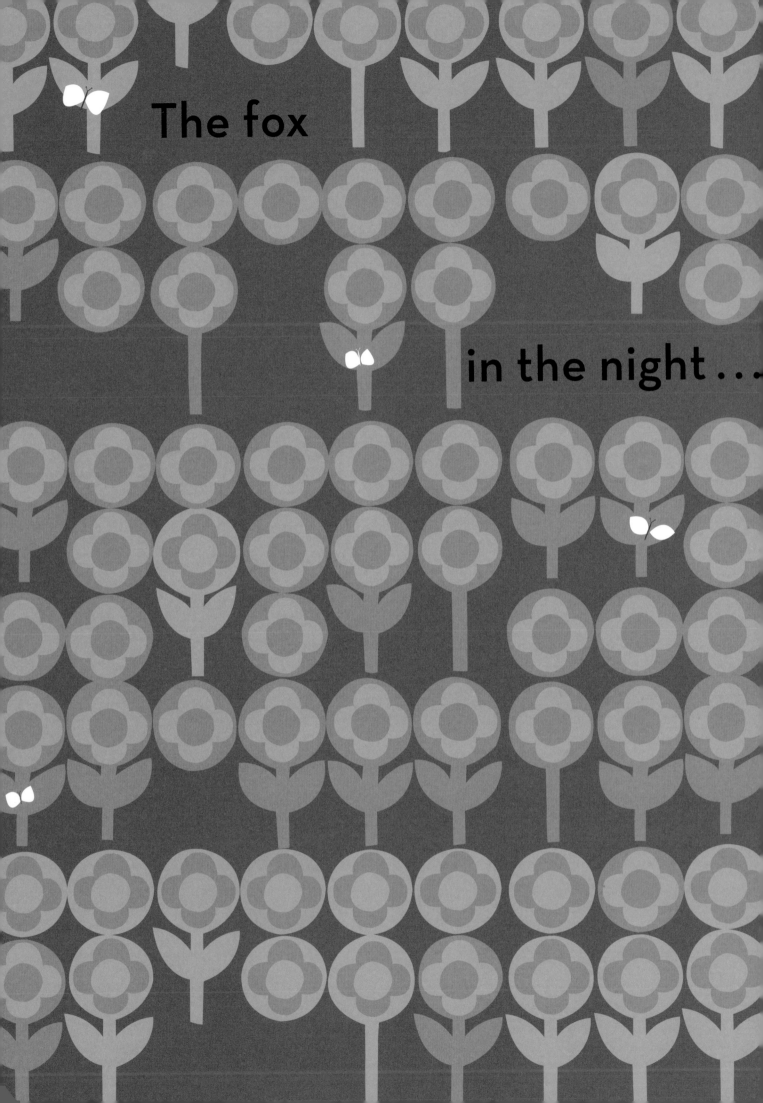

The fox

in the night . . .

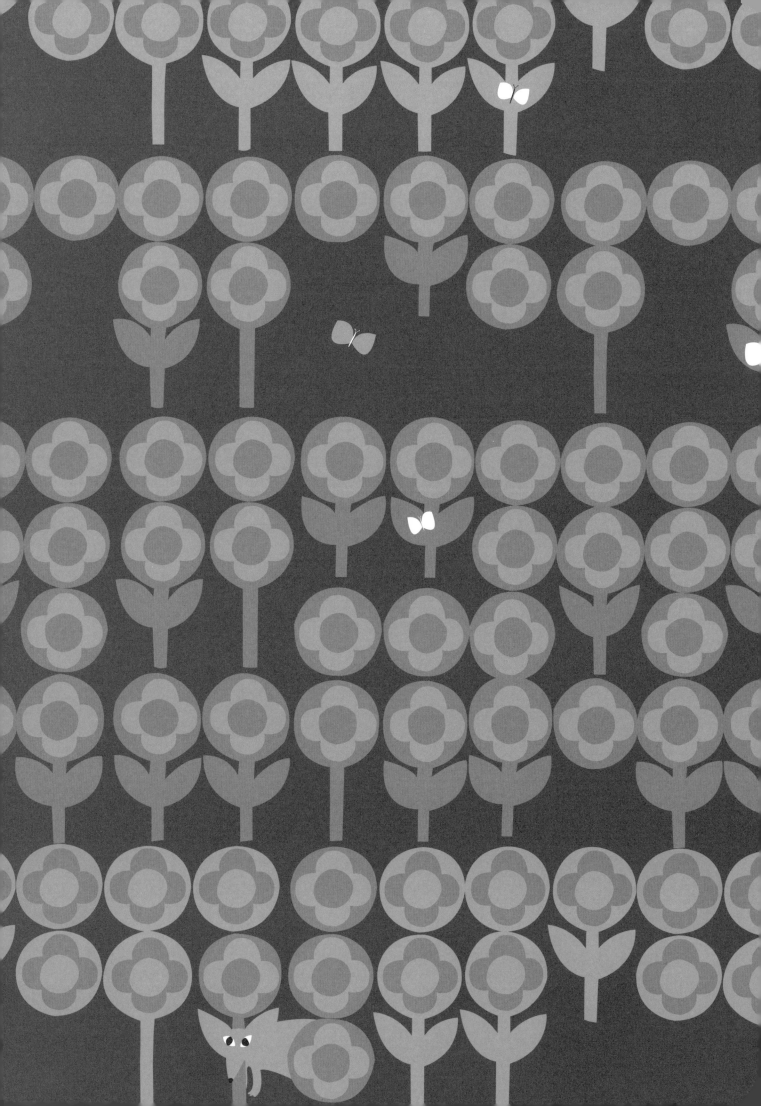

The stunned snail . . .

The farm girl
in the forest of fir trees...

The ladybug with five spots . . .

Father sea urchin and his son playing hide-and-seek!

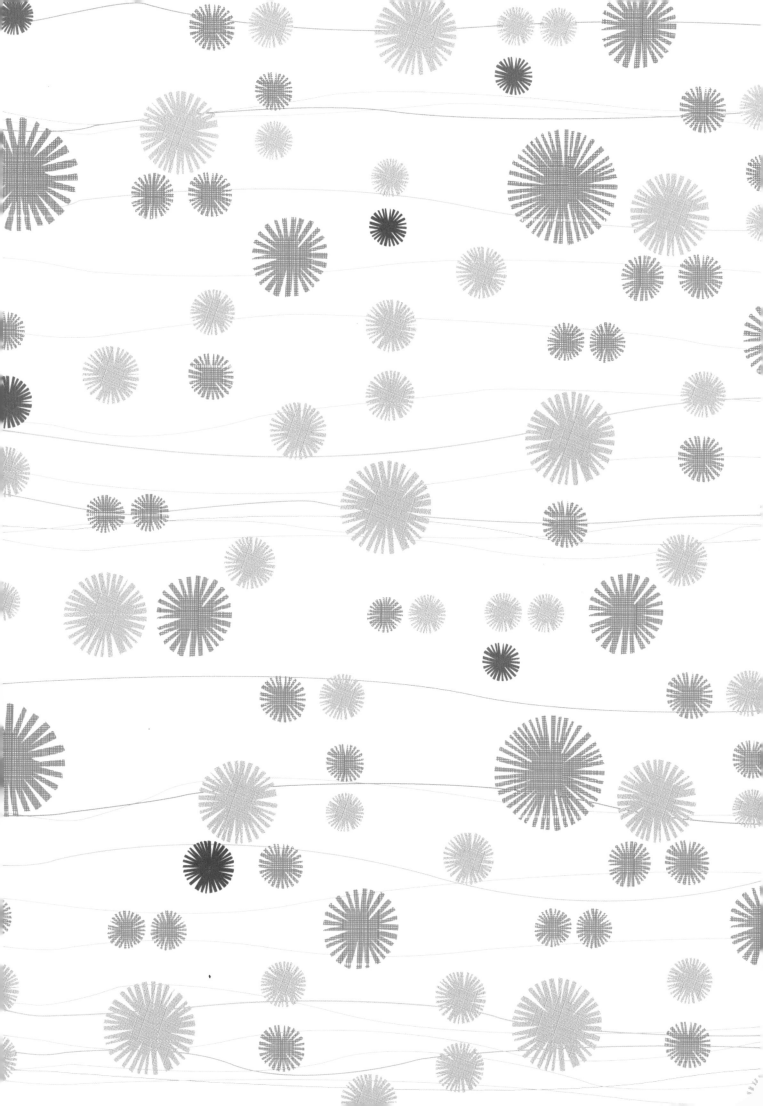

Find the bee
ready to gather nectar …

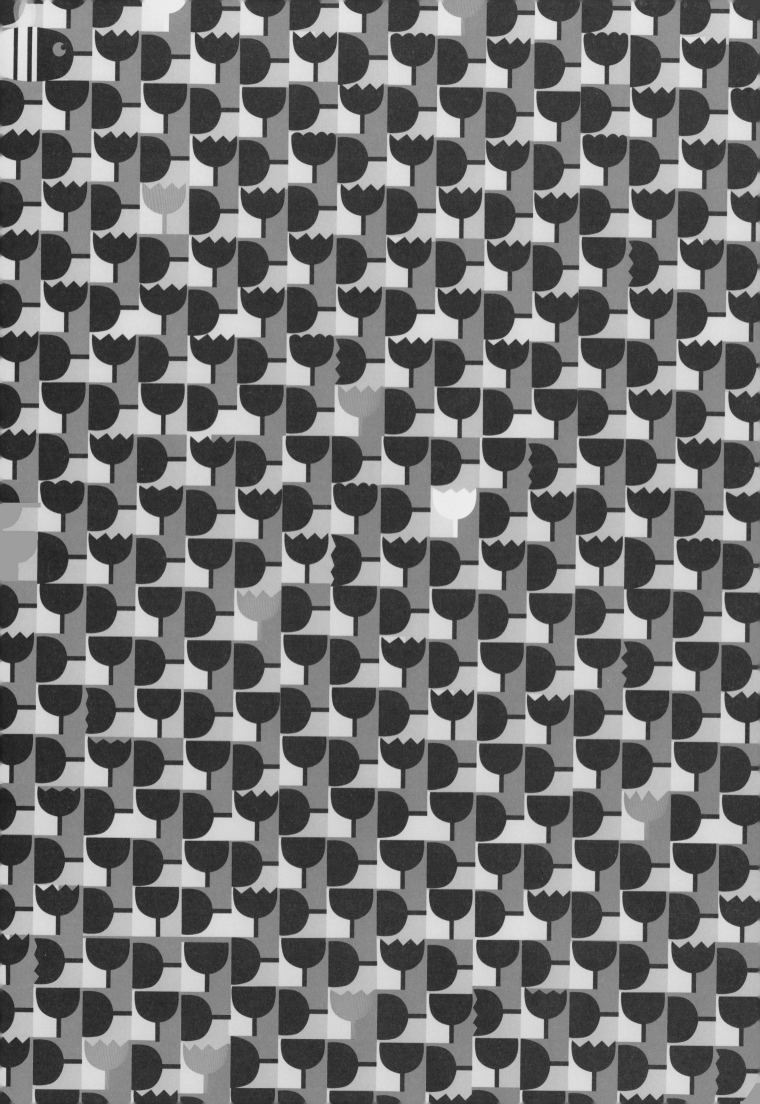

The butterfly
searching for a flower . . .

The earthworms
playing soccer ...

Mama, papa, and
wee baby bird …

The hamster
who lost her ball . . .

And the
tightrope-walking stick insect.

Look! Most of the little creatures are hidden in the forest, but one of them has lost its way.

Which one is missing?